ANNA PERRY

GINA'S DIRTY CURVE

dark fantasy adult romance books

Contents

1.

    1.

2.

    1.

3.

4.

One

Chapter 1

MY BRAND-NEW STUDIO APARTMENT

I've completed unpacking at last. I set a photo on the window sill by my bed and take a quick look around my new apartment. An empty bottle of Cava and two vintage champagne flutes, leftovers from our celebrations the previous evening, are placed next to the plant that Jane purchased for me as a moving-in gift. This portion of the apartment already appears cramped due to the bed, two book stacks, and a protruding clothes rail. Between the "bedroom" and the "kitchen," a used sofa serves as a partition. It is furnished with a coffee table, three deep purple floor cushions (taken from the cafe from which I work), as well as a 1970s kitchenette that I absolutely can not wait to redecorate.

This is my brand-new studio apartment, which is home to everything I own. It could appear pitiful to a stranger, but to me it's ideal.

I eventually ended my three-year relationship—which should have ended much sooner—with my lover three months ago. I've been couch surfing ever since I moved out, so having my own space feels amazing. I don't mind paying the higher rent for a studio apartment because I've been craving this opportunity for such a long time. Now that I've finally landed a respectable career, it's time for me to also have a place to call home.

With my ex, the previous year was intolerable. He had always been envious, but his possessiveness grew more oppressive as we drifted away. In order to avoid receiving fifty snarky texts and having to convince him that no, I hadn't danced with any boys and yes, it had been a terrible night without him, I would have to "forget" my phone if I went out without him. I stopped wanting to see my closest friends because of how horrible it got; even a night out with Jane would end in an argument.

But cutting off communication with Jack was the biggest sacrifice I made. Jack was my closest friend, but Jane is the oldest. When I was a waitress at his father's restaurant on Saturdays, I initially worked with him. On my very first shift, he made me laugh, and ever since then, we have been inseparable. We always sneak away on our breaks with bottles of half-finished wine and taste each course "just to make sure that it's OK for the customers." I had no idea that my weekend employment would influence my future profession. However, I already knew that my crime-partner would become a lifelong buddy.

One of those breathtakingly attractive men that every lady wants to go out with is Jack. He's had a run of attractive, uninteresting girlfriends for as long as I've known him, which is predictable. *Try telling my ex that we are simply friends; there is nothing between us.* We got into so many arguments over Jack that I stopped seeing him and let our relationship utterly deteriorate.

Okay, there was a moment when I questioned whether something would transpire between us. Together, we had traveled to Spain to stay with his aunt. Long, leisurely days on the beach drinking cool beer with innumerable bocadillos were so much pleasure. In our eight-year friendship, it was one of the very few instances that neither of us was in a committed relationship. In actuality, I had just come to fill in for a girlfriend he had split up with a few days earlier.

He dared me to go skinny dipping the night before we left for home. We were seated on the pier at one of the restaurants' tables that had been set up close to the water. I immediately took off my strapless dress because I knew he thought I'd never do it and I was more than a little inebriated. I then dove right in. I squealed as I raced to the surface through the ice-cold water.

Jack was rolling on the floor laughing. He grabbed me in his tanned arms as he reached down to lift me out of the water, and an electric current flowed between us. I wasn't wearing a bra and noticed that my little underwear was see-through from the water when I climbed up to him. Naturally, I felt embarrassed, but as his gaze swept over my body and rested on my nipples, I nearly forgot about it. I wanted him to look at me because I thought this was the first time he had truly noticed me. I felt a surge of excitement pour through me as my thighs tingled. I don't know for sure, but I got a strong feeling that he would have kissed me if we hadn't seen the waiter come over at that very moment.

We sat back down to finish our drinks as soon as I put on my outfit, but the ambiance had entirely altered. We had been laughing uncontrollably and making fun of each other every other night. We suddenly fell silent, as expectancy filled the space between us. I recall being both thrilled and angry that this was just occurring now, the evening before we left for home.

He again put his arm around me as we made our way back to his aunt's apartment, but this time it felt different and more tentative as his fingers delicately circled my sun-kissed shoulder. My senses were more acute, and my heart was racing. My hair was covered in salt water, which mixed with his skin's delicate perfume. The sound of music and conversations in the restaurants we passed made the humid night air feel as though it were about to engulf me. Everything was surreal and heightened. My vision was of me sitting on the edge of his aunt's dining room table while he stood nearby kissing my neck, pulling my fancy dress up to my waist, and going inside of me. Jack, my closest friend, is biting down on my breasts while sucking the salt water off of my skin.

However, none of that was intended. We arrived to find his aunty and a room full of neighbors and friends waiting for us. We immediately returned to our usual roles as Gina and Jack, wholly platonic friends, in front of this multitude of people.

The fact that he was lying there in the next room, tantalizingly close, kept me from being able to fall asleep that night. He appeared to be as sleepless as I was, struggling with the cover while naked in bed. I was unable to endure it; I had to let go of the need he had sparked. Jack's powerful hands going up my thighs, his hot, hard lips, and his soft, moist tongue inside of me were in my mind as I put my fingers between my legs. I pursed my lips and grasped the bed covers. I experienced a shuddering orgasm as the hard, dense idea of him pulsed through my body before dozing off in frustration.

Two

Chapter 2

MY BEST FRIEND IS BACK, WHAT'S GOING TO HAPPEN NOW?

As Chris and Ben exit the cafe and head into the pitch-black night, I kiss them farewell and lock the door. They have earned their tips after a long, demanding day of work, demonstrating to each client the enthusiasm in which we take great delight. I wouldn't settle for the wage increase the owner offered me when he said he wanted to stand aside and start a new business; instead, I ran through my suggestions for renovations and insisted on becoming a shareholder. Although it's a small sum, it has a significant impact. My sense of investing my energies in someone else's effort has subsided. I'm doing this for myself, and it has given me the courage to make changes in my life.

I proudly cross off the modifications I've made as I make my way through to the tiny rear office. I have a wall set aside for local artists to display their work, and it is always changing. I saw Jack's father in a painting of a proud, moustachioed man with warm eyes. At the work computer, I go on to Facebook, looking forward to the mindless diversion that will help me unwind after a long day. I visit Jack's profile page by clicking on it and go through his photos. Recently, this has developed into a habit, and before I know it, I've wasted thirty minutes looking at photos of Jack with bikinied females on a beach in Thailand, Jack riding a motorcycle while seated across from a friend, Jack's trademark, endearing grin, and Jack haggling at a market. A live message from the man himself, "Hi stranger," then appears in the corner of my screen.

Does he realize that I'd been stalking him? I blush shamefully.

Me: Hello, how are things in Laos, Thailand, or wherever the hell you are?

Him: Back at Cassa Davidson, he said. But thanks, they were all fantastic.

Me: Oh my God! You are at home? I've put my shame behind me since I'm so happy to see my old friend.

Him: Of course I am. Do you wish to meet soon?

Me: Yes, I would love to. Too much time has passed. You need to arrive as soon as your jet lag has subsided. I currently reside in Holloway and work at McMadison, a charming tiny cafe that you will like.

Him: "I heard." After more than a year, Gina, I still miss you.

Me: I know; I also miss you. I'm very sorry I missed your departure; back then, everything was a chaos. When can you come over? Tuesday?

Him: I may need to assist at the restaurant because I'm strapped for cash, but I'll let you know.

Me: Amazing, can't wait. XX

Him: I don't either.

I take a confident step as I make my way to the bus stop. The way Jack makes me laugh, his unexpected shyness if I ever manage to make him flush, and the midnight feasts we'd prepare after a night out have all been much missed. I've been kicking myself for letting my ex's ego overshadow our friendship. I've now realized how pointless it was. He would not have had faith in me regardless of what I did or did not do. And Jack is the first man I've ever truly, amicably gotten along with. Well, mostly straightforward.

The following day, I have the day off, so I spend it wandering around the Market. Halloumi with chorizo, apricots, and a green bean salad strike me as the ideal combo when I consider what to get for Jack when he visits the café. I try to imagine McMadison from his perspective. Now that I'm finally able to realize my dream of owning my own restaurant, how will he view me?

I carry my new items back to the bus after locating a mirror, a cashmere throw, and a box of wine glasses for the apartment. A tall, tanned man with a huge bunch of sunflowers is standing at my door when I arrive at my building. It's Jack, and he's beaming at me.

I casually drop my luggage at my feet and put my arms around him as he murmurs, "House warming gift."

"Thank you, oh my goodness. How did you discover my residence? You appear really good. These are so lovely "I sob, feeling overjoyed, frazzled, and completely shocked.

I contacted Jane and asked for your address after going to your café and finding you there to be absent.

We are now ascending the stairs to my apartment. I'm balancing my bags and the flowers. Jack presents an uneasy appearance, as though he is unsure of what to do with his hands.

I welcome him inside my studio but immediately get uncomfortable.

I apologize, "I've just just moved in, there's still a lot of work to do on it.

It's fantastic, Gina, he exclaims. He is focusing all of his attention on me rather than the surroundings.

I tell him, "You're gorgeous." not "You look good." also "How are you?" The truth is the only thing I can think of. He's bigger than I remember him being, more muscular and tanned; he seems to fill the entire apartment and towers over me.

He doesn't say anything, but holds my chin in his palm and brushes his thumb along my cheek. I shiver. I'm not sure how to respond because I don't want to disregard this gesture and ruin the occasion. I want to lean against his strong, warm body. I don't recognize the Jack I recall. He might appear both strangely familiar and completely unfamiliar and fascinating, which is perplexing.

He whispers, "I've missed you."

I hurry to give him a hug because I can tell how much he means it, but as I do, he gently lifts my face up and gives me a full-mouth kiss instead.

At that point, I'm broken. My hands rush up to his face and I give him a quick, passionate kiss as my hunger surges to the surface. He responds to each of my kisses by luring me in and placing his hands under my T-shirt, bringing life to every square inch of skin. He pushes me to the ground while simultaneously undressing and kissing me as we eagerly pull off each other's tops. He stops, kneeling above me, his chest rippling above the waistline of his jeans, while I get all the way down to my pants and extend my legs to him.

He brings my foot up to his mouth and kisses each of my toes as he adds, "I've waited so long for this moment, let's not rush it." He glides up the inside of my legs, touching my thigh with his cheek while licking and kissing it. He exceeds my wildest expectations in every way. He inserts his fingers inside of me as he kisses my stomach, and he groans, so he must have sensed how excited I was.

He says calmly in my ear, "Gina, you're very lovely.

I can sense it. more lovely than I've ever experienced in my life. I'm expecting him to go further and deeper inside of me, so my hips are raised off the ground. In response to each of my groans, he taunts me by pulling back with a stroke and coming in again until I'm about to scream.

I try to pull on him by reaching into his jeans, but he keeps saying, "Not just yet, Gina, not yet." He waits until I reach, waves of ecstasy rushing through me, then turns me over onto all fours and pulls me up onto his lap so that I'm kneeling with my back to him while keeping his hand still inside of me. I anticipate him to remove his hand, but instead he continues to carefully stroke me, slowly extending his fingertips while his other hand squeezes my breast and kisses my back all the while. I feel another orgasm coming on.

When he removes his hand, I'm still clenching and releasing in pleasure. He has taken a condom out of his wallet, as I can see when I turn around and look over my shoulder. How did he know to bring a condom has me scratching my head. Did he intend for this to take place? Instead of feeling angry as I had anticipated, I became even more aroused.

He moves inside of me, his hands on my waist guiding my movements. Although it's completely overwhelming, I also don't want it to end. I turn around and wrap my legs around his waist, holding onto the nape of his neck and gazing into those stunning blue eyes of his. He grunts and accelerates while saying, "Oh God," forcing me back onto my elbows so he can reach forward and kiss my breasts.

When I notice that he is going to orgasm, I am so excited and filled with want that I climax once more, holding him tight as we tremble together.

Jack carefully strokes my legs while placing his head on my stomach as we recline on the carpet. We both feel too fatigued to speak, and I wouldn't even know where to start because there is so much to say.

After remaining motionless for fifteen minutes, he raises his head up on one elbow, looks at me, and smiles.

I chuckle, "I can't believe this is happening."

"I realize it's absurd. When I was away, I really missed you, so when I learned that you had split up with your ex, I was deeply affected."

But as we have been lying there in quietness, my thoughts have been racing. I'm not prepared to start a new relationship just soon because I don't know Jack's plans or even where he will be living. My best friend has recently returned, and I don't want to lose him again. But the thought of us reverting to being friends again and him getting a new girlfriend is enough to make me uneasy.

"Jack, what will take place? I've missed you so much, but I can't let our friendship suffer because I can't let you go again. And I need a little bit of this space, this time, to myself. However, you can't just walk in and start acting this way and expect nothing to change. I'm not sure how you will take this, but everything will change."

He puts a finger to my lips, quietly saying, "Gina, slow down." "I agree. Likewise, I have no idea what I'm doing. Just now have I returned from my travels. I only know that I've wanted this to occur for a very long time."

I hesitantly inquire, "Since Spain?"

"perhaps even earlier. And before we begin to doubt this, there is a long list of stuff I would like to do with you "He says as he lightly touches my lips.

I feel a knot of anxiousness start to dissolve in my stomach right away. I cross over and rub his strong arm.

Then, what else is on this list? I merely ask.

He gets to his feet and helps me stand. He leans in for a long, deliberate kiss while cupping my bottom in his hands. He starts to tighten up against me, and then he quickly lifts me off the ground. I automatically wrap my legs around him. He begins to recite his ideas about us in between kisses and bites on my neck.

"I want you in the shower, on that coffee table, on every surface in your café, kissing every inch of your body, tasting you, outside, in my car, on that Spanish beach, watching you touch yourself."

He throws me onto the bed, and I moan.

I balance myself on one elbow and slide my hand between my legs while keeping my gaze fixed on him.

I answer, feeling more self-assured and sexual than I've previously felt in my life, "Let's begin there then, and when we've crossed everything off your list…"

It's a pretty big list, he says, so "don't worry about that."

Three

Chapter 3

Before Gina boarded his train, one man believed that this business trip would involve nothing but work, work, work.

I had been chosen to attend the annual shareholders meeting on behalf of my company. I am currently bundled up on a train. The surprising aspect? Regina, our latest trainee, will be working with me. I'm not exactly sure what she will be able to contribute, and now I have to watch the kid instead of relaxing. It was going to be a real pain in the rear this weekend. All I needed for the icing to be a train strike.

I'm sitting at a table on the train and am facing an open seat across from me. Good, I think. "Stuck with Little Miss Unreliable, who might even fail to show up before the train departs. It fits me.

I spread my legs out to unwind and begin the newspaper reading when a small redhead comes up and starts fumbling with what appears to be crucial papers. She drops the papers, and I stare at her with a blank expression on my face. As I assist her in picking up the papers off the floor, I audibly sighed.

She flings her copper red hair out of her face and introduces herself as Regina in a light voice.

She stumbles as the train jolts forward, and one of her legs flies in my direction. She is wearing her short pencil skirt with straps, which I can't help but notice. With an extended arm, she balances herself on the back of my chair.

I smile and say, "I think you should sit down before you fall down."

I raise my feet off the chair, and she cautiously takes a seat across from me.

"Ok, Regina… Do you anticipate the shareholders meeting?

She almost whispers, "You can call me Gina." I see the most stunning brilliant blue eyes as she combs her hair behind her ears and glances at me through her glasses.

Okay, Gina.

She cuts her off with, "Not really. To be completely honest, "I was expecting for a leisurely weekend with a few glasses of wine."

This was an intriguing turn of events, I suppose. I had this preconceived notion that I would be saddled with a dull, overeager intern who was just interested in conducting business.

I respond with a smirk, "I'm sure we can find time for a few drinks.

I attempt to seem to be somewhat interested in what she has to say as we chat for the next hour or so of the trip. I have to admit that it became harder and harder for me to ignore Gina's bulging cleavage as she strips away the top few buttons of her thin, white blouse.

She abruptly exhales a huge sigh and takes off her high shoes.

She put her feet on the chair next to me and groaned, "My feet hurt." She says in a humorous way, "Rub them better for me.

"I can't do just that," you say. That is baseless… I could

Gina tuts as she fiddles with her hair. She then moves her feet from next to me and places them in the space between my legs before abruptly beginning to rub my crotch.

I find it shocking. Completely dumbfounded and unsure of how to respond. I am aware of my obligations. I should be polite and remind her that we are on a business trip while also moving her feet. But the devil in me won't allow it to happen.

As I stroke her legs, her foot keeps rubbing my already hard cock. How much more time will this journey require? I feel like I'm going to blow up.

We flag down a taxi as soon as we arrive at the station and get inside. I pass the taxi driver a torn piece of paper with our hotel's address written on it without saying anything.

I gently push Gina's lips against mine as I grab hold of the back of her head. I hurriedly add, "I've been dying to do that the whole train ride."

We have a passionate kiss during the taxi ride, and when we get to our hotel, I barely even say "thank you" to the driver. Sincerely, I believe he enjoyed seeing us from the back seat. I give him the cash, and then we immediately cross the street to the hotel and check in. Gina's hand has been massaging my protruding pants the entire time we have been waiting at the front desk.

Both of us dash upstairs and meet in my room. Gina has already taken her top off by the time I've set our bags down, allowing her red hair to fall over a silky blue push-up bra with black lace edging. I pause and take in the breathtaking scene that is right in front of me for a moment. Her tiny frame was practically screaming at me.

I approach her and push her back against the door by grabbing both of her shoulders. One hand grips her tits while the other struggles to untie her bra as we kiss furiously.

She doesn't spend any time slipping a hand down my pants and freeing my cock.

She clutches my throat and whispers to me in a passionate voice, "Don't get too soft with me," as we hurriedly peel off all of our clothes and throw them on the floor before running across the room to the bed.

I flip her over onto the bed, parting her legs with mine as I climb up on top of her. I seize her wrists and hold them against her head on either side. I bite at her neck as I lean in to kiss her collarbone. She begins to raise her arms from the bed as soon as I let go of my hold on her wrists. She is once more restrained by me as I shove them back down. I hold her hands together with one powerful hand as she raises them above her head. I grab one of her firm, full breasts with one hand while still holding the other two in place. Her skin is a delicate white. My hand moves over her toned stomach and down in between her slim thighs while sucking and chewing on her nipple. She is wet as I run my fingers over her pussy. She responds abruptly when I stick my fingertip inside of her by saying, "NO!" I'm confused, so she notices and says, "I want your cock to be the first thing inside me."

She immediately grabs the back of my head and thrusts her tongue into my mouth when I stroke her clit and let go of her hands from above her head. She leans forward while I lean back, trying to keep our lips together.

How tough should I be, I wonder? …

She lies on her front when I turn her over. "Punishing you is in order!" As I speak, I can feel myself assuming a more dominant position.

I place my right hand—which I've just retracted—against her beautiful, fair skin. My hand striking her solid butt creates a high-pitched cracking sound that pierces the air.

Yes, she groans. "Again." Her skin changes color from porcelain white to scarlet red as I repeatedly whip her buttocks. I swing one last time and grab her butt as my palm touches her scarlet cheek.

I position myself to be straddle her legs. Her pussy is wet with eagerness, and I can see it shimmering in the light. I'd like to sample it. Once again, I flip her over onto her back, but before I can act or speak, one of her hands flies forward and seizes my head.

I know you want to, she whispers firmly as her fingers encircle my hair: Take me. She thrusts two fingers into my mouth so I can taste her by sliding her hand between her thighs, then she raises her hand back up. So delicious is the flavor. She can tell in my eyes that I want more.

I get pushed down by her.

She groans, "Lick me."

I comply with her request immediately and start licking her crotch. She's drenched, and as I make her scream loudly and more, I can feel myself working more and more.

Her body twitches with pleasure as her breathing becomes louder and heavier. I simply pause to nip at her inner thigh. Her perception is sharper, and as I bite her, it nearly feels like her body melts.

I want to feel you inside of me. She says while beaming broadly.

I turn to face her as I pull myself nearer her. She takes hold of my cock and slowly pulls it in her direction. I maintain my position while the tip of my penis touches her, not moving a muscle.

Then I move myself closer to her as slowly as I can. My cock slowly moved farther inside of her. I wish I could freeze this emotion in time.

So that she may feel every part of me inside of her, I eventually go as deep as I can. Her vagina tightens around me and grabs me. It feels wonderful. I'm almost lost in her eyes at that precise moment.

As I bang her tirelessly and quickly while still holding her in my arms, I lift her up and carry her over to the wall, forcing her against it. I must have found the sweet spot because I felt a gradual ejection of pressure on the tip of my dick.

She moves her body and pulls my dick out while squirting.

I slowly move in and out of her again while sliding my cock back inside.

Remember you can squirt once more? I ask.

"Yes! She leaps.

I help her to the floor before jumping back onto the bed and motioning for her to follow. She mounts me and begins to ride. Once more, I can feel the pressure increasing.

"FUCK!!" As she cums, she yells loudly.

"Your turn now,"

I get up as she gets down on her knees next to the bed. She gently strokes my balls while slowly sucking my erection. She notices how my leg jerks and how much it hurts. I rage. I grin as I say in a hushed voice:

The best business trip of all time

And it's still not over, big boy. She chuckles.

Chapter 4

GINA ENCOUNTER WITH THE ARTIST

Two thirty. He'll be set to go. Damn.

In an effort to hide the tops of my stockings, I wriggle my dress down.

In an effort to preserve the cosmetics I painstakingly applied less than an hour before, I spray cold water on my neck.

So be it. That will have to do. I smear on red lipstick till it is thick and sticky on my lips. 'Alarm'. His preferred color. I adore the routine I go through to get ready for him. the illegal rush. the fearful anticipation of what he may do to me. Does he intend to look this time? He's going to touch? There could be more. Or will he simply paint while smoking a cigarette and ignoring me as I burn for him?

He throws open the door of the taxi, which is already waiting at the agreed-upon meeting place.

He blindfolds me as we start the car, and we go silently to his studio. I have never been able to find it there in all my visits.

When the blindfold is taken off and we arrive at our destination, we are in a familiar place. From all sides, sleazy individuals in varying states of undress and sensuality glare at us. His works have a sumptuous, almost carefree vibe with hot, ominous undertones that make me think of the 1980s.

"Step forward." He gestures at a wooden pillar with his hand. He takes off his jacket and cuffs his shirt.

I settle in and turn toward the easel.

"Remove your top half," He said.

His voice is scratchy and thick in that way that suggests a life spent smoking and drinking fine whiskey. Or does he consume brandy? I get a thrill from the thought of the lingering decadence aroma on his breath and skin, even after a bath. He exhilarates me. a man's "fuck you" attitude when informed what he may and cannot do. I enjoy it. He observes me as I undress, his pussy quivering as he licks his lips and breathes thoughtfully. I try to unhook my bra by reaching behind my back, but he extends his hand.

"No. Forget it." He gives me, my form, a cold, calculating look. Although there is no human-to-human feeling there, he is so intent on the subject as an artist that I feel an overwhelming urge.

What do I need, though? What draws me to him, exactly? Never has he touched me. Never once. Furthermore, I've never even seen a sketch. He merely sends me on my way after we am through, smoldering. As he focuses on my chest, his brow furrows. My nipples ache and peak as they clamor for attention.

I hold my breath as he moves forward with both palms extended, reaches in over the top of my bra, and loosens out my breasts. I allow my head to drop back as he pulls more firmly because of his chilly touch. As he continues to work, I swing back and forth on my heels until both tits are at their leisure. He is able to fold each cup's top half into itself so that it looks like a balcony. Perfect. Did he really rub my nipples between his fingers and thumbs, or was it all in my head?

Oh, the heat and drenched yearning he would discover if he ran those artist's fingers up between my thighs. one touch All it would require is that. I may be sent spiraling into that wonderful region of oblivion with just a small circle of a finger tip on my clit. However, he doesn't. He goes and I'm left here. Each and every hair stands up and reaches out to him. My entire body is screaming, yet I'm mute. As he motions for me to go to the side of the post, his gaze is fierce.

He draws the wrists together while pulling my hands around the pillar and forcing me to arch my back. He goes slowly. Always, he does. He once took an hour to position me since, according to the scene, a few millimeters mattered. This time, he's not just speaking to me; he's also touching me. I feel as though I'm in a dream.

He asks me to hold onto my fingers as he searches through a crammed drawer and returns with a length of strapping. It resembles shreds of a torn cotton sheet. My body starts to shiver.

He continues, "I want you uncomfortable this time," with a trace of an apology, as if to emphasize that the painting, not him, is the one who desires it. I consider, then reconsider, as though there is a difference. Perhaps that is a different aspect of him. An interdependent dark twin.

In response, I move my heels apart and stretched the already-taught fabric until I hear a hemming stitch pop. His deep throat groan of approbation spurs me to press on, my legs trembling under the strain and confinement.

He ties the strapping after pulling it tightly around my wrists. My forehead and chest start to perspire, and my hands feel clammy. I'm a little ashamed of how hot and worried I am. But I'm helpless against this onslaught of arousal.

He approaches and Stand in front of me.

I let go of the strain in my knees as I slump slightly and sink into the pillar. He is approaching now, and I hear myself squeal. He turns my head to face him while clutching my hair in his fist.

I prepare myself for harsh remarks, but instead, he reaches into my exposed neck, takes a big breath, licks the back of my throat, then tongs my collarbone like it's my c*nt.

God, oh God. I intend to attend. His other hand is rubbing and massaging my nipple while simultaneously drawing it to a point and releasing it. My chest is heaving, and my head is still held in his grasp at an awkwardly divine angle.

He rolls and suckles on my other nipple as he moves to do so. My pussy is burning up. I picture my bodily fluids oozing out over the tops of my thighs like lava. While still clutching my hair in one hand, he immediately releases my breast and thrusts his hand up my skirt. I lose my footing but am kept up against the post by his strength. He is roaring into my neck with his mouth back at the base of my throat as he dips a little. As he rubs me, I can just just make out his curls. My inside thighs' soft pillows are squeezed by his fingers, which he then slips into my underwear and pulls out to the side.

I'm now moaning. As he inserts his fingers into me and pulses, fucking me frantically, my head reclines. My pussy is moist and spread, and he pumps quickly. His thumb makes a circle just above my clitoris, around the rigid top of my vagina. He exerts considerable pressure. It's a strange feeling. Unusual, almost uncomfortable, but good.

I picture the scene: me with my skirt tucked, with his forearm and elbow pumping between my legs. Who would understand his depth? Who was to say how much I could handle?

When he relieves the pressure on my pudenda, I have an odd sense of blood returning to that area, which makes me throb with need. *As his thumb finally touches my rumbling clit, I whimper.* Oh, I agree. I hump my pelvis into his hand while rocking.

I murmur, "Yes, yes, harder," in a jumbled, shaky voice. I feel that way. Fractured. He fractures me as he hard fucks me with his fingers. continuously breaking apart. My neck tenses as the shuddering begins. He grips my hair even more tightly as I attempt to move forward in the typical orgasmic position. I briefly became anxious. He is unaware of my peculiarities. I must arrive with my chin drawn in. The way things are. However, he twists his thick, deft, artist's fingers in my c*nt at such an odd angle that I surge and burst, leaning back while biting down and convulsing around them. He holds me till the shaking stops and a weird ache replaces it.

He slowly and carefully backs away, shutting me up once more and adjusting my head. I can see his cock squeezing through his pants as he stands.

I give it a nod.

Do you want me to…? I mumble.

While wiping his hand on a rag covered in paint, he shakes his head and grabs his brushes.

As he hides behind the easel and starts to mix the paint, my heart is still pounding.

He always hands me a piece of paper that has been folded up with instructions for our next meeting at the conclusion of our sessions. He does not bid us farewell. He simply takes a big suck on his cigarette as he stares intently into me through the taxi window.

As the cab pulls away, I raise my hand to wave, but he's already turned. In the gutter, the cigarette butt is smoldering.

I unfold the note to find out how long I'll have to wait till the next time while the sway and lurch of the cab journey hypnotizes me. It can take weeks or even months at times.

I spread the paper out on my lap as my breath starts to catch. Time and date are not present. No assurance of a future Just a lovely, unfinished sketch. An uneasy and sensual woman is fastened to a pole while she is turned away.

THE END...